THIS CANDLEWICK BOOK BELONGS TO:

_____

_____

_____

For My Very Own Father — who, if he were a dog, would
of course be a most intelligent, witty, and dignified breed
E. B.

For Dad, of course! And the dogs, as with every dog
I have ever drawn, are for Mom.
R. C.

Special thanks to the ever-cheerful, patient, wise Joan Powers — and to
Randy Hilarious Artist Cecil, to Liza, Anita, Kate, Elise, Ellen, Phyllis, Jane, the Zoo, Liz,
Tiff, Will, and Jake, and most of all to cheerleader Josie, the Rose Princess.

Text copyright © 2006 by Elizabeth Bluemle
Illustrations copyright © 2006 by Randy Cecil

First paperback edition 2008

The Library of Congress has cataloged the hardcover edition as follows:

Bluemle, Elizabeth.
My father the dog / Elizabeth Bluemle ; illustrated by Randy Cecil. — 1st ed.
p.   cm.
Summary: A young girl suspects that her father is really a dog because
he performs such acts as fetching the newspaper and chasing balls.
ISBN 978-0-7636-2222-0 (hardcover)
[1. Dogs — Fiction. 2. Fathers — Fiction.] I. Cecil, Randy, ill. II. Title.
PZ7.B625254Myf 2006
[E] — dc22   2005054285

ISBN 978-0-7636-3077-5 (paperback)

2 4 6 8 10 9 7 5 3 1

Printed in China

This book was typeset in SoupBone.
The illustrations were done in oil.

Candlewick Press
2067 Massachusetts Avenue
Cambridge, Massachusetts 02140

visit us at www.candlewick.com

My Father the Dog

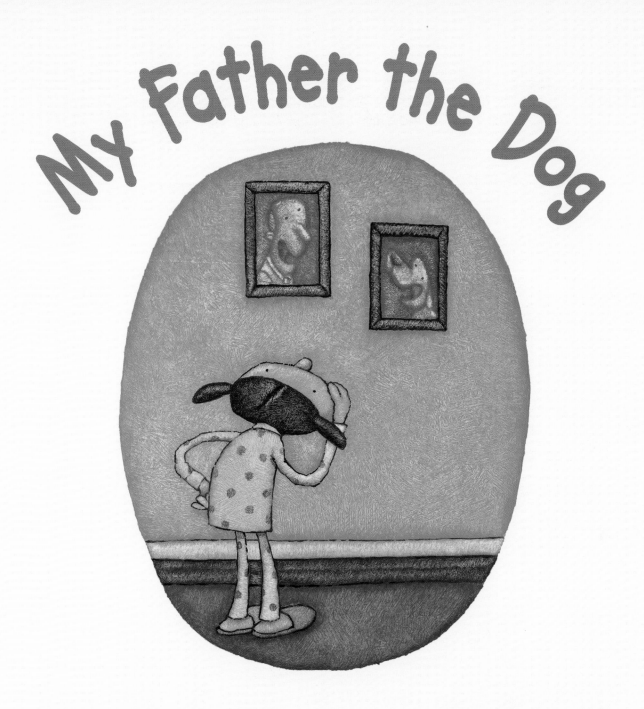

Elizabeth Bluemle   illustrated by Randy Cecil

CANDLEWICK PRESS
CAMBRIDGE, MASSACHUSETTS

My father pretends to be human,
but I know he is really a dog.

Consider the evidence:

When he wakes up, he's fuzzy around the edges.
He starts off the day with a good scratch.

He fetches the newspaper every morning.

My father loves to roughhouse and play tug of war.

He hates to lose.

In the car, he likes the windows down and a breeze on his face.

He has been known to use a
tree for a quick pit stop.

My father can lie around for hours.

He growls when you startle him out of a nap.

If you throw a ball, he'll chase after it.

My father loves snacks.

I've never actually seen him begging for scraps under the kitchen table, but it could happen.

When he toots, he looks around
the room like someone else did it.

He is good at looking innocent when
he knows he's done something wrong.

If he hears a noise in the middle of the night,
he runs downstairs to investigate.

My father is loyal and thinks we're
the best family in the world . . .

which is good, 'cause Mom says we can keep him.

Elizabeth Bluemle co-owns the Flying Pig Bookstore in Shelburne, Vermont, with stand-up comedian Josie Leavitt. She holds a master of fine arts degree in writing for children from Vermont College. *My Father the Dog* is pure fiction, she says. "This book is not based on my own father. Honest, Dad, it's not."

Randy Cecil is the illustrator of numerous books for children, including *And Here's to You!* by David Elliott, *We've All Got Bellybuttons!* by David Martin, *Looking for a Moose* by Phyllis Root, and *One Is a Snail, Ten Is a Crab* by April Pulley Sayre and Jeff Sayre. He is also the author-illustrator of the picture books *Gator* and *Duck*. Randy Cecil lives in Houston, Texas.